T0147764

Poetry, Songs And Stygian Stories

Written by Lucas McPherson
Illustrated by Cyan Jenkins

iUniverse, Inc.
New York Bloomington

iUniverse books may be ordered through booksellers or by contacting:

iUniverse
1663 Liberty Drive
Bloomington, IN 47403
www.iuniverse.com
1-800-Authors (1-800-288-4677)

ISBN: 978-1-4401-9530-3 (sc)
ISBN: 978-1-4401-9531-0 (ebook)

Printed in the United States of America

iUniverse rev. date: 1/4/2010

Poetry

1) Real Time & Sex
2) Sometimes Sappho
3) Popular Culture
4) Landbound
5) Always an Indie Author at Heart
6) Some of the Powers
7) Dissipating the Entropy
8) Emo-Vamps
9) Hypocrisy

"Real Time & Sex"

Real Time and Sex are over-rated
By-products of Ego, over-inflated.

I don't care what you ate,
Especially when a meat-meal.
Or when you last shit, for god's sake,
For I don't like it when you're that *real.*

I frequently like time delays to focus on my art;
Not spend most of my time talking about nothing
Right now; that doesn't bring any comfort to me,
Nor does having sex & then bragging about parts.

"Sometimes Sappho"

I used to frequently amuse
Myself, saying I was like the 10th Muse

Always...with limited Y-Chromosomes around
So as to not be purely hormone-bound.

Yet, later I chose to be mostly around one with a Y
Though another path might have been easier...
Why?

Well, because being with Xs only, for me, is so very
Feasible.
Though I wouldn't have had all the dear contrasting
Conceivables...

That aid in my writing; my authoring mainly from
plenty of differing viewpoints, seldom one.

It's through massive immersion in at first foreign
Awareness.
That's caused me to grow at a rapid rate, and to
report on both sides, as an Equalist, the
Unfairness.

“Popular Culture”

A supposed Wise One
Critiqued another’s love of

A pop culture figure today.
For in his superior-sounding

Knowing of facts, not wisdom,
He said that a particular icon

In today’s time
Was in reality from

What he called mainstream staves
From centuries ago, by gods,

Then wasn’t that the majority of people’s
Popular icon back then?

"Landbound"

Plastic bottles I always pick up along the way
They are my faux seashells, wind whistling away
Through them as I act out my own plays…

Over the hazy asphalt roads, jungles, ceaselessly
Sun-dazed and Sun-burnt each and every day.

While the wished for waters roar in my ears,
As I imagine oceans of salt water---
No salty tears~~~

I'm stuck in suburban mediocrity:
Swimming in the dried up middle-class sea~~~

Looking at other green lawns manicured to a tee;
Yet, they have no recycling for pick-up like me;
They love their stagnation, honing complacency.
And I'm stuck in their drama, not wanting to be.

"Always an Indie Author at Heart"

Don't expect me to follow your protocol
Just to facilitate your way.

Inherently, I'm an Indie Writer,
Who follows only what I say.

Perhaps you mistook me for
A pedantic highbrow author

And such, but I can assure you I'm not, for
I prefer hardcore---not hairsplitting & fluff.

"Some of the Powers"

By Bastet, I believe that my greatest claim
Is to understand the purr-fect cats of mine.

There are Spirits, too, but only when asked for
Not uninvited, with other animal-folk of fur.

Plus, I gave permission in love success to be mine,
But only because my Partner desired this as well;
Forever we are entwined, no need for love spells!

However, I only advise those I feel like helping;
Emotional Vamps, all demanding, are sent hiking
Past me, for I don't fuel their futile dead fires;
They should seek their own ways out of the mires.

To those who are despairing though,
I try to support & ease their load.

Gladly sharing treasures of knowledge with them
Always brings prosperity and shiny gold ends...
Perfectly punctuated with all the lovely gems***

“Dissipating the Entropy”

I had to dissipate the entropy in my own system
Because the old methods were no longer working.
So, I found new methods before I went berserk.

Used to be drinking to excess was one way,
When I didn’t want to grow, only play.

Or when I worked incessantly, refusing to look
Inside for fear of what I’d see; I was hooked
On quick fix habits, instead of bravely facing
What I, after time, chose to: inner analysis
Of me, I found I had to let new concepts be
Inside of me. Brief pain, then world altering
Adjustments are great when allowed patiently…

RIP

“Emo-Vamps”

Emo-Vamps are the worst kind
Constantly sucking up---Never mind
It’s not your blood;
It’s even worse---‘Cuz

They’ll suck all your life-force out
If you let them with their dramatic pouts
And always placing the blame on everyone
Except themselves! They hate you having fun…

They want you to wallow with them in the mire
Of self-absorption and general lack of desires.

So, if you have a *friend* like this,
Then cut them loose & let them piss~~~

Away their sad existence with their own kind:
Don’t give them your happiness & peace of mind!

“Hypocrisy”

You said *bathroom humor* was beneath you;
Yet, a stranger gave it to you in the *pooper.*

You said I should blindly follow your way;
I said I have my own---no need to pray!

You think you’re superior ‘cause of your bloodlines;
I think it’s an excuse not to excel in your own times.

You’re only vindicated by a walled-garden society;
An almost dead one that’s refused to grow,
you see.

Truth is: you’re not able to make it on the outside;
As you won’t face your own fear, you merely deride.

It’s not a fault of mine that I don’t respect you;
I don’t value cowards, or call yellow blood *blue.*

Songs

1) Not Listening
2) Pitiful Mother-In-Law and Cheating Father-In-Law
3) My Grudges Got Too Heavy

Not Listening

Chorus: **Your Spirit likes to hang around me**
Because in your death, I'm the only
One that can hear you, but I'm not listening.

So, just go away today, at least, anyway
As I'm filled now with the memories
Of how you never heard me
When you were still alive.

Chorus: **Your Spirit likes to hang around me**
Because in your death, I'm the only
One that can hear you, but I'm not listening.

So often when you were alive, I tried & tried
To be heard, but you just turned a deaf ear
To all I'd accomplished---that much is clear!

Chorus: **Your Spirit likes to hang around me**
Because in your death, I'm the only
One that can hear you, but I'm not listening.

Even in Spirit, you're still in a pitiful state
Of insecurity and well-practiced hate.
For, still you don't acknowledge my brightness;
Even though the world has surely witnessed it.

Chorus: **Your Spirit likes to hang around me**
Because in your death, I'm the only
One that can hear you, but I'm not listening.

Pitiful Mother-In-Law and Cheating Father-In-Law

Chorus: **Dwelling in stupid overcast hazes**
Where old *mourning* glories stay open all days~~~

They were the worst examples
Of how married life should be:
You see, the M-I-L wanted to divorce the F-I-L
But was too scared of trying life her own way.

Chorus: **Dwelling in stupid overcast hazes**
Where old *mourning* glories stay open all days~~~

The fat F-I-L came onto his own daughter-in-law
At the booze-flowing wedding celebration one fall…
Saying she used to be his type,
Like he stood an incestual right
To be with her.

***Chorus:* Dwelling in stupid overcast hazes**
Where old *mourning* glories stay open all days~~~

F-I-L felt his Ego's right to be with her
Because she'd married the better part of him,
In one of his sons, but such prurient thoughts
Were unbecoming of old men and fruitlessly dim.

***Chorus:* Dwelling in stupid overcast hazes**
Where old *mourning* glories stay open all days~~~

They tried to rule their grown sons' lives
Because they had never developed their own.
Yet, she once fell into the trap of pitying them,
Till they tried to force her back in their fold
To hone their lording over ways on him as well;
So, she and her love had to leave that place,
Where the other son and his wife still dwell~~~
In the putrid Padres stagnant & personal Hell…

Chorus: **Dwelling in stupid overcast hazes**
Where old *mourning* glories stay open all days~~~

My Grudges Got Too Heavy

Chorus: My grudges got too heavy
So I simply let them go.

My days were lost in dull and hazy
Depression, as I focused on them so

Much and such. Now I crave
Freedom and flight, the cleansing light

Except when I write and recall
Drama-ville, duplicity, and passing the ball.

Chorus: My grudges got too heavy
So I simply let them go.

Now I take responsibility for what I create
In my life, so I won't hang with Drama Kings
Or Queens; instead, I create fun-filled Scenes…

Chorus: My grudges got too heavy
So I simply let them go.

Stories

1) Karma's Bitch
2) What Really Happened in the Labyrinth
3) Cellulitopia (Microfiction)
4) Vampire Meet
5) Here, Kitty Kitty
6) S.O.B. Charlestonians
7) Preeminent Parts
8) The Final Frontier (An Explicit Sketch)
9) From Vegetarian to Vampire

RIP
RIP

Karma's Bitch

I can't believe I'm in this graveyard! I didn't mean to do it. It's just that that bitch was getting so uppity. Forgetting she was my old lady and shit. I didn't mean for my punch to kill her. I wasn't aiming for her temple; she stupidly turned her head; I would have just broken her nose. If she hadn't told me with her hands on her hips that bitch meant b.eing i.n t.otal c.ontrol of h.erself, then I wouldn't have done it. But that bitch dared to tell me some kinda bullshit like that. I pushed her down the stairs after I killed her, making sure she hit the broken baluster where I'd pushed her before, and I made sure the spindle lodged in her temple so it looked like an accident. The stupid cops bought it. Only thing is: I thought I saw a neighbor close her blinds in the apartment across the street right after I'd covered my tracks. She might have seen me kill her, too.. I plan on paying that bitch a visit soon.. Make sure she never speaks, in case she saw something.

Shortly after reminiscing, Richard Dittmar, his friends called him Dick (a.k.a. the killer in this story), watched with no expression on his face as his wife's body in the casket was lowered into the

ground. He was so eager to leave the graveyard before having to talk to any family, etc. that he almost tripped over a pregnant dog near the cemetery gate. Angered, he kicked the poor dog in the belly. She whimpered away as he hastily left showing no concern for the pregnant bitch.

The asshole Dick Dittmar got in his beat-up pickup truck, the only one on the street with rednecky dirty balls hanging below his license to show the world that he was a real man, and drove back to the place he used to share with his recently-murdered wife. He figured he'd put back a few beers and then see about taking care of that busy-body neighbor who might have seen him do in his better half.

Morgaine was holding her poor dog's head in her lap. Her doggie Molly had accidentally escaped from the apartment while Morgaine was sleeping during the day, and Morgaine didn't even realize that Molly was missing till she awoke that evening. Morgaine called for Molly everywhere in her apartment before setting out to find her. The only place Morgaine figured Molly might be was the cemetery where she first met the stray, four years ago, when she'd gone to pay her respects to a loved one in the graveyard late one night. Morgaine had taken her home, and they'd basically been inseparable ever since.

Morgaine was crestfallen to find her poor Molly laying on a grave of freshly filled dirt, whimpering and unable to move, as she'd prematurely gone into labor. Molly looked up at Morgaine with such pain in her big brown eyes, that Morgaine immediately sank to the ground by her side and took her furry head in her hands gently. *Feel better now Molly* she thought over and over again hypnotizing Molly with her eyes. It was working. Molly stopped whimpering, but her labor couldn't be stopped. All her puppies were born so prematurely that they didn't make it. Morgaine buried them under an oak tree in the graveyard. Then, she lifted Molly tenderly and took her back to their apartment. Morgaine's long nails were still packed with graveyard dirt when she heard someone knock at her door.

Dick had downed close to a half case of beer when he decided to pay a visit to the bitch who might have seen him kill his wife. He knocked rudely about ten times in a row. He was insistent she open up. He had an unregistered gun in his pocket; he planned on using it before the night ended. He was sure he'd have no problem overpowering the bitch. He figured he'd get her out to his truck by threatening to shoot her and then take her somewhere out of town, then really shoot her and then bury her body.

Morgaine opened the door, surprised to see some big Redneck reeking of beer standing there. Molly started growling at him from across the room. "Easy girl," Morgaine said soothingly, now eying the stranger warily. She was picking up on the vibes of her dog, who was always a good judge of character. The man boldly stepped over the threshold without being invited in and headed towards Molly, thinking she looked liked the pregnant bitch he kicked in the graveyard. "No, that can't be the same bitch," he said, getting closer to Molly with each step.

Alarmed for Molly's safety, Morgaine alluringly spoke to the bold redneck with, "Why don't we go outside for some fresh air?"

"Even better than that, why don't you and I go for a ride Hoth Thang?" Dick slurred, happy that this was going a lot easier than even he expected. Plus, he was pretty sure he'd get some good sex out of the deal first. What he considered "good sex" would be considered rape by most. Dick couldn't believe his good luck! They got into his filthy ride, the balls swinging from side to side when Morgaine shut her door, and they headed out of town. Dick was about to ask Morgaine if she'd seen anything unusual from her window the night he killed his wife when Morgaine suggested they pull over by a large ditch. Dick was so excited that she'd chosen that spot, that he was grinning broadly exposing half rotted teeth stained a tobacco brown-yellow. He leaned in towards Morgaine trying to force a kiss on her lips, but she'd had enough right about then. She'd already been able to pick up on his thoughts…the ones where he'd killed his wife, intended to kill her and worst of all, the thought that sent Morgaine over the edge, kicked her pregnant dog causing her to lose all her puppies. The thought of Molly's pain rehashed in her mind, and it turned Morgaine's eyes red with anger and her to thoughts of vengeance. Morgaine could readily read most human thoughts when she tuned in. She was definitely what most humans called psychic; it came with the territory when one was a vampire. She'd had enough of the presence and inane talk of the redneck. She head butt him when he went in for the kiss. He was sent back stunned to his side of his vehicle. Then, she quickly fed on the vein at his wrist as he sat back still dazed from her head butt. Then, she quickly broke his thick red neck, pleased at the gratifying snapping sound. He never really knew what was going on. He

could just feel himself being jerked out of his now lifeless body. For a minute he floated above his body, then he saw some grey forms around him pulling him against his will and throwing him into some kind of thick black sludge. It was thicker than mud, more like tar, he remembered thinking before he felt his etheric body's flesh burning off the bone in the tar-like substance that only got hotter and hotter till it burned with flames across its surface. When the former Dick had no ether-flesh even attached to his soul, he went somewhere else where he was told he'd shortly be reborn.

. . . . .

Morgaine wiped the stupid redneck's blood from her mouth, and she then opened Dick's door to make her exit. She had a long walk back to her apartment, and she had to make sure she'd arrive before sunrise. But, before she left the truck, she walked around back for her souvenir; she quickly ripped off the truck's dirty balls and started her trek back to her apartment.

. . . . .

The irony wasn't lost on the former Dick as he felt the fur covering his body. Only he wasn't

a he anymore; he'd been reborn as a female puppy. And his only sustenance came from the bitch, his mother. One moment he was at her nipple drinking and the next he felt himself being jerked away from her and carted somewhere. He was put in a crate and shipped to a dingy restaurant in the midst of people's voices, but he didn't understand the language they were speaking. One moment the chef was peering at him menacingly and the next he saw a shiny cleaver overhead.

• •

Ernst, Dick's former father-in-law, was still mourning his daughter's death. He knew in his heart that that son-of-a-bitch husband of hers had murdered her. Though Ernst never once stopped to think that she probably wouldn't have married an abuser if he hadn't abused her terribly as a child. No, Ernst didn't blame himself at all. He was excited that he was about to enjoy a delicacy, to drown his sorrows, that he'd flown half across the world to get; it was illegal in most places. Forget dog, he was into only tender puppy meat. And within moments the puppy formerly known as Dick was served up to his former father-in-law, arriving piping hot at his table.

What Really Happened in the Labyrinth

*****This short story was published in *Psychic Times International* at http;//www.voicesfrombeyond7.com/PsychicTimesWelcome.html in their Fall 2009 Issue, and it was also published in the Samhain 2009 Issue of *The Witches Digest* at http://www.witchesdigest.co.uk**

My father, the king, was always railing against the Cretans for one reason or another. And, the worst blow he felt he could ever deliver to me was to call me a Cretan, in his frequent fits of anger over things he thought I'd done wrong. His most recent tirade had come about after I'd informed him that I'd become a Vegetarian. Contrary to what he adamantly believed, it was by no means to upset him; rather, it was simply because I hated the idea of eating meat. My father was super miffed because he considered it a demonstration of disrespect to not eat all the animal flesh he'd hunted and brought home for all his family and palace crew to feast upon. Moreover, I wasn't alone in choosing not to consume animal parts: my six best male friends and my seven best female friends, who were part

of our castle crew, had also decided to become Vegetarians a little while after I had. My father was livid at that news, too, especially since it came so close on the heels of my own. He felt that I'd influenced them into becoming Vegetarians and had therefore usurped his wishes. At that time, I remember him pitching a fit, as demonstrated by him throwing his hands up in the air while at the same time pacing back and forth before screaming, "You're all Cretans! No decent Athenians refrain from ingesting animal flesh! What's this?! Are you and your friends turning into cannibalistic Cretans?!"

"Father, please calm down. It's not like that at all. For one, Cretans haven't eaten human flesh for years, and secondly, it just seems wrong to me, an Athenian, to eat animals."

"Wrong? I'll tell you what's wrong!! Wrong is empathizing with the animals!" And with that, he stomped over to his bear skin rug and kicked the poor expired beast in the head, for emphasis in his mind, I suppose. It just seemed a cowardly move to me, to kick an animal that'd already clearly fallen. Then he started his verbal assault again with, "Next thing I know you'll be telling me that the Minotaur, a Cretan who still eats human flesh, by the way, is just a misunderstood beast. Try telling that to the

fourteen dead Athenian youths, who lost their life to his hunger last year!"

I didn't dare say, at that point, that I *did* sometimes think that the Minotaur was indeed misunderstood and that his eating human flesh could perhaps be explained. I mean, if I'd been the Minotaur and had had my own grandmother, the fine Brown Cow, served up for all those sitting in the dining hall of King Minos' palace, then I might have gone a little berserk as well. Especially since King Minos had expected his step-son, the young Minotaur, to eat with everyone else seated there, including King Minos' wife: the Minotaur's mother, Pasiphae. Pasiphae was eating the mother, the fine Brown Cow, of the beautiful White Bull she'd mated with to produce their offspring: the Minotaur. Pasiphae was eating the Minotaur's grandmother, right in front of her son, yet Pasiphae had no problem with it. And, no one else seated at the royal spread seemed to have a problem with it either, except the Minotaur's half-sister, daughter of King Minos and Pasiphae: Ariadne. She had a big problem with eating the animal flesh of her half-brother's grandmother! It seemed barbaric to her, so she took a stand along with her half-brother, the Minotaur, in not eating the Brown Cow. However, King Minos couldn't be defaced

by his children in front of the other guests dining there, by their refusal to eat the Brown Cow, so he felt he had to punish them!! So, King Minos had his architect, Daedalus, build an elaborate labyrinth to put his step-son in for punishment. The Minotaur was to meditate in the labyrinth for years on how illogical he'd been in not partaking of the royal food set before him. Plus, the Minotaur had also gone a little crazy at that royal dinner by eating some of the king's guests who were heartily feasting on his grandmother. Feasting on some of the humans who'd eaten his grandmother was quite logical to the Minotaur in an eye for eye kind of way. At least he'd shown restraint in not eating his own family!

King Minos was a lot more lenient when it came to the punishment of his own flesh and blood, his daughter Ariadne. He gave her several clews, threads, to weave into a royal robe fit for a king, which was a near impossible task since she was given such coarse threads. Ariadne hated her father for making her do that and for imprisoning her half-brother in the labyrinth just because they'd done the right thing in not eating the Brown Cow.

But, I digress, so let me get back to my own conversation with my father, the King of Athens, who was also known as Aegeas. Regarding my being a Vegetarian, I said softly to him, determined to remain rational and calm, "Times change Father."

"Really? I suppose you'll be saying next that I no longer have to sacrifice fourteen Athenian virgins, male and female, to the Minotaur yearly to keep us from being attacked by the Cretans because he's become a vegetarian now." He laughed out loud while saying it, but his eyes betrayed the anger he felt for me as he came mere inches from my face to spit out, "Tell you what son, you go as one of the fourteen to be sacrificed to the Minotaur this year since you feel so strongly for the beast and believe in the supposed Winds of Change." I looked at him in disbelief for a second; he was, after all, a father that would sacrifice his own son to appease his own pride. I'd always found him to be verbally abusive (and, if it weren't an anachronism of sorts, then I'd even say he was a gaslighting abuser), but this turn of events? It was brutal, even for him. He tried to sugar coat it a bit later with, "Fly the white sail when you return son, so I'll know you survived." But I secretly thought, *If my life is spared by the Minotaur, then I'll be sure to only fly the black flag, so that perhaps my father's own guilt will destroy him; he deserves it.* So, that's how it truly came about that I (Theseus is my name by the way) and thirteen of my good friends came to set sail for Crete.

When the fourteen of us landed in Crete, I was singled out by a lovely girl toting a big ball of coarse thread. Turns out she was none other than Ariadne! She quickly explained that the Minotaur was her half-brother, known to her as Asterion. She insisted I take her ball of thread with, "Tell Asterion that you were given this thread by me, and he'll be more likely to listen to you, if need be; plus, it will help you find your way back if you unravel it as you walk." Ariadne was more than happy to find other, more important, uses for her clews, besides making a royal robe for her father. Believing in her sincerity, I carefully tucked the ball away and smiled at my brave Vegetarian crew. Not long after that, we were marched to the opening of the Labyrinth. A large door was opened and we walked inside the enveloping darkness. I immediately started unraveling the thread as we steadfastly walked forward into the unknown. I could hear Ariadne shout to me from the other side of the door now, "I'll wait here for your return!"

Forging forward, sometimes scraping our arms and legs against the walls of the elaborate maze, the fourteen of us knew it was our destiny to meet the Minotaur. Known as a beast at best and monster at worst to most. But we weren't most. We all felt like giving Asterion the benefit of the doubt. After all, he was really a victim himself. For his mother was forced, by the vengeful God Poseidon, against her own will (many would call that black magick) to fall in love with the White Bull, his father.

It wasn't long before we saw glowing red orbs in the near distance. My thread had been unraveling steadily and was perhaps about half-way unwound at that point. We kept on walking forward toward the lights till myself and a few others bumped into a wooden table of some sort with various objects on top. We all must have jumped back about a foot when we heard a deep voice simply say, "My altar."

Much as I would question one of my friends, I asked of him, "You have an altar in here?! For…?" I started.

"For my shadow magick rituals since it's always dark in here, even in the broad daylight outside."

"Oh, I thought it might have been for…," I began.

"For my human sacrifices?" the Minotaur kind of snort-laughed, genuinely amused.

"Well, you have nothing else to eat except the humans you've been fed for sacrifice, right?"

"Yes, that's been the case for quite a while, but they have nothing to do with my shadow magick rituals. And, look...about the eating humans thing. I find it pretty disgusting myself. About as disgusting as eating animals. But I wanted to survive. So, I did. It didn't bring me any pleasure; in fact, it made me sad. I tried to kill them quickly so that they wouldn't feel much pain. Plus, I consoled myself somewhat by the fact that they were all humans who'd consumed animal flesh throughout their entire young lives. I could smell them and tell; their bodies gave off an aroma like the graveyards of dead animals to me. But, you fourteen are different. Your scent is lighter; you don't smell like death."

Making him out to be about 12 feet tall in the limited light, I looked up at him and answered, "That's because we all made a choice a while back to become Vegetarians. We made a decision to respect our Animal Friends."

Bending down to get closer to my face as if to study me more, the Minotaur replied thoughtfully, "I see that you are telling the truth and have true honor. I will not kill you all then; it doesn't seem right to kill such as you." It occurred to me then that Asterion, the Minotaur, was more logical than most Cretans and Athenians in the outside world. And it seemed to me that he'd probably grown wiser through his lengthy introspection in the Labyrinth (because he had no outside interference).

"It certainly wasn't right that you were supposed to eat the meat of your own grandmother, the Brown Cow," I stated with growing empathy for him.

"True, and I suppose it did drive me crazy trying to figure it all out for a while there. I still don't have the answers for why it all went down, but now I simply don't care as much. I'm tired of trying, to tell the truth. I've been grateful for the solitude of this Labyrinth, for the opportunity to frequently meditate and for the soothing darkness. But, I'm ready for a change now. My life here has served its purpose. It's shed light on the darkness of many truths. Follow me now!" the Minotaur gently commanded as he grabbed something from his altar. "And hold onto my tail, it's long enough for all of you, so you won't get lost in the darkness." Then his red demon-like eyes shone the only light for all of us as he led us to the very center of his home. It was there we all quietly circled around him. Don't ask me why we did. We just felt compelled to. He didn't look like a monster to us; rather, he looked like a weary creature we wanted to comfort. We saw his very human chest rise and

fall with labored breathing. Then he slowly said, "I'm tired of this life, my friends. And, I'm happy to end it soon surrounded by noble souls like you." And with that, he took his athame (that he'd removed from his altar) and plunged its double-edged blade deep into his heart. With his dying breaths he managed to say to me, "Tell them you killed me, or my step-father won't respect you and let you leave. And, please tell Ariadne thanks for taking a stand with me; you two will be very happy together…" And with that, his epic body collapsed to the ground with a great reverberating sound. Then we all saw a large bright light, like a huge glowing orb, shoot out of his chest through his self-inflicted wound. One of my friends carefully took his horned head into her lap as she tenderly caressed his lifeless cheek. Instead of being the taurine terror that most thought him, he'd sacrificed himself for the fourteen of us in a sense. Moreover, we all saw that his true form was that of a bright and shining star. I decided from that point on that I'd only refer to him as Asterion. And when I became king, so would all in my kingdom***

Cellulitopia (Microfiction)

I worked in the worst place a fat girl could possibly ever work: a strip club! Oh, don't get

the wrong idea; I wasn't one of the dancers in a forward-thinking club where the patrons were all *chubby chasers.* No, I unfortunately worked in the standard thin-girl-type-strippers strip club. I was a waitress there. I worked at the heinous kind of club that encouraged girls to go under the knife and endure suction tubes, etc. for a kind of thin-girl-curvy, in what they considered the right places, versus my own kind of natural misshapen fat. My boss, a pot-bellied asshole with a receding hairline, had complained to me about my weight umpteen times, to no avail. He would have surely fired me a long time ago if I weren't so good at my job. I got patrons their drinks the quickest because I was never asked to stop and flash my fat, in not the right places, boobs. It didn't bother me too much that I was the most efficient, yet I always went home with the least amount of money. At least I was still making decent money. Besides, it was easy to just show up and do my job. I was used to the brainless rote conversation; I liked not having to concentrate hard while I was there. My mind was always free to wander, so while other parts of my job sucked (like not being acknowledged for being uniquely beautiful), I had to admit I liked being able to space-out while working. . Yet, with no real challenges, I didn't feel at all fulfilled.

Perhaps that's why I liked to overindulge in food. At work, I mostly day-dreamed of other worlds, other places. Somewhere else in the whole Universe had to be more fulfilling for me than Earth. I'd, of course, heard of parallel universes; in fact, I'd studied up on them quite a bit. One of my favorite theories was that when we sleep, it's not our subconscious mind having its say; rather, it was that in sleep, we're traveling to parallel universes.

One night, as I fell asleep, already deep in a theta waves state, I wished with all my might that I'd find a place where I'd be valued most of all and challenged in just the right measure… and when I awoke, I was no longer on Earth. I'd arrived in Cellulitopia where my localized lipodystrophy was to be proudly shown off like a trophy. There were no plastic surgeons to remove the lovely fat deposits as they were considered beautiful. Though it's of note that I now live in constant fear of falling asleep for fear I'll return to Earth.

Vampire Meet

I'm kind of bored. Just passing the time watching a palmetto bug sickly crawl in an off kilter fashion and then kind of barely fly, spreading his shiny black wings only partially as if too weak to do more, over the algae-covered- cement-over-brick covered wall in St. Michael's Graveyard. Looks like the big flying cockroach, for that's what palmetto bugs are, was unfortunate enough to come into contact with some kind of bug poison. I have to wait till I can meet my family at dusk in the family crypt at Magnolia Cemetery, and I can find nothing better to do than observe this infirm roach and recall my family's past. The rest of my family can't stand the sunlight anymore, but in the well-worn- in-my-memory past, we used to hunt for plastic Easter eggs filled with candy. We'd hunt for the eggs as a family, in St. Michael's Graveyard, back when I was a child. But things have changed a lot since then, for though we still hunt, none of us have the same taste anymore.

. . . . .

I'm the only one in my family of mostly vampires now that can still go out in the sun, so I take care of our old antebellum house's upkeep, see that all the bills are paid, etc. I was born human and so were they, but we all started turning in the year 2000. While most of the world was concerned with major computer bugs, we'd caught a more deadly one. One that those of our particularly isolated genetic bloodlines were more susceptible to, when those less isolated weren't. The rest of my family never admitted it, but I think it had something to do with Southern Aristocrats marrying their own cousins back in the 17th, 18th and 19th centuries. Even though we didn't know for sure what caused it, the symptoms of the *bug* were unmistakable. We started off merely photosensitive, but then we became photo intolerant. The sun's rays would burn most of my family to a crisp now. But not me anymore. Something had started to change...again...with me. It was strange; I was no longer in danger of becoming a crispy vampire critter, but damn my ancestors anyway for all their sinful inbreeding! Though the rest of my family had changed somewhat since being turned by the *bug*, they haven't adapted into what I've become. Rather, they morphed from being humans, to vampires, to now what

I'd consider vampire ghouls. My family went from vampires that just subsist on human blood to those that like both human blood and human flesh. And me? Well, I've changed so much that both human blood and human flesh are no longer appealing to me. Yet, I still hunger…

••••••••••••••••••••••••••••••••••••

It's finally twilight, and I'm quickly making my way to meet my family at Magnolia Cemetery. More truly blue-blood Charlestonians are buried there than in any other cemetery some say. My family certainly qualifies, but they're not the kind that have stayed buried. They're probably waking up from their dead-like sleep right now. I miss the old life we all shared: from all of our private school educations, travel abroad, the St. Cecilia Balls, the church music (but not the tedious readings from the male-dominated Christian bible and snooze-inducing sermons) on Sundays, the brunches at the Carolina Yacht Club, etc. I still crave that old way of life at times in fact, but not as much as my current craving; I'm so hungry now, but I'm no longer craving human blood and/or flesh…

••••••••••••••••••••••••••••••••••••

I don't usually fly in stealth mode when entering my family crypt, but I am for some reason right now. I'm not sure exactly why. Mommy's already awake. I can see her sarcophagus is open, and she's brushing her long blonde hair. Daddy's stone sepulcher is just starting to move. Soon my brother and sister will be stirring from their death-like sleep as well. All of the sudden, I feel acute hunger pains welling up within me. What am I hungry for? First I hungered for human food, then for human blood, then for human gore, but now? What is this fourth hunger? I no longer feel my *normal* vampiric cravings. What is it I'm craving? Blood, that's it after all...and flesh....but wait! Something's changed. Something's different. I see the vein pulsating in my mother's neck...pulsing with her now blue-black blood. Yummy! And the curve of her creamy neck...intoxicating! Now I'm starting to understand. I stay in stealth as I fly beside her, smelling her sweet vampire meat. That's it...I'm thirsty and hungry for vampire blood and meat!!

Here, Kitty Kitty

Michelle kind of regretted her decision to move to *The Big Apple.* She was born and raised a country girl in South Carolina after all, and to say that her life now, living *Up North*, was different was a gross understatement. When she first heard that New York City was called *The Big Apple* she was excited because she figured the place just had to be filled with lots of fruit-eating Vegetarians with a moniker like that! She was really disappointed to later learn that New York City was filled with just as many meat-eaters as her rural birthplace was. It had been challenging, to say the least, to be a Vegetarian when the rest of her family was a bunch of country-fried-steak-loving-bacon-on-almost- everything-pack-of carnivores. Yet, she'd somehow managed to be true to herself, despite their best efforts to get her to be like them.

The only thing Michelle had taken from her home in the *Deep South,* after securing her job with an alarm (security system) company in New York City, was a big, beat-up suitcase and her cat, Lamia. The transition to life in New York

City seemed harder on Lamia than on herself, but they'd managed to cope. Michelle had already rented a small apartment, about the size of her bedroom back South, so it was good she'd thought ahead, but it was depressing for both her and Lamia to live in such cramped quarters. Plus, she hated that it had only one window to look out of that revealed only another taller building across the street and the filthy street itself below. Still, Michelle considered herself lucky: she wasn't forced to live on the street, and she'd beaten being just another redneck statistic by not staying in her hometown.

However, Michelle's world was turned upside down when Lamia went missing about two months after their moving to *The Big Apple.* Michelle was more than distraught at the thought of her precious fur ball surviving on the tough New York City streets alone. But Lamia was happier being outside, at least happier than being cooped up in their small apartment. Michelle did everything she could think of, including putting up lost cat posters and even knocking door-to-door to see if anyone had seen Lamia. One day, because Lamia started to miss her human mistress, she decided to return to Michelle. Michelle heard her meowing outside and quickly opened the door and scooped up her precious Lamia, not caring that there was blood matted in her long grey fur. Michelle didn't care because the blood didn't belong to Lamia. If it had, then that would have been a different story.

Afraid of losing Lamia again, Michelle made sure their window was closed at all times, for that's how Lamia had escaped, and Michelle soon started looking for another job. She figured if she worked two jobs then she could afford a bigger place and then Lamia would be happier and not want to run away again.

Plus, Michelle wanted her second job to be one that paid well, as she was hoping to get some new furniture, save for the future, etc., too. Because Michelle hadn't been raised in a family where lots of job skills or even a college education were valued, she didn't have a lot of options. So, she decided to become a stripper. She remained a Security System Consultant by day, and she became a Stripper by night.

The day she and Lamia left their small apartment for a larger one, she noticed lots of skeletons of dead rats in the street gutters near their moving truck. Michelle looked at Lamia calming licking her paw in her traveling cage, and just shook her head.

Working two jobs enabled Michelle and Lamia to furnish their new much more spacious apartment, closer to Central Park, with lots of lovely new furniture for Michelle and elaborate scratching posts/cat gyms for Lamia. And, they had two big bay windows to look out of in different directions; Central Park could even be seen from one. Life was great now for them both!! In fact, they'd been in their new place about six months before anything really eventful took place again. That particular day, Michelle had finished her day job as security consultant and had about two hours before she had to be at the strip club to dance. Being a practicing Pagan, she'd already lit her white working candle and was getting ready to light her green and red/gold candles from its wick (for major money-bringing since it was a waxing moon). Green candles bring about quick money and the red/gold (Taurus) candles bring about long-term wealth. She'd also carved sigils into her candles before lighting, and she also burned some parsley powder and ginger root powder on her charcoal tablets for both protection and even more money flow (for/to her). But all that burning made her apartment quite smoky, so Michelle had to open one of her windows. Something she hadn't done since Lamia escaped from their other New

York apartment. Fortunately, Michelle opened the window near the fire-escape stairs because Lamia jumped out of it quickly (without looking due to being so excited to get out). It wasn't just the smoke that cause Lamia to flee, it was also the desire to have more freedom and the fact that the energy Michelle had raised, from her candle magick rituals, was making her nervous. Lamia had moved so quickly that she looked like one big grey blur.

Not again! Michelle thought, dismayed. She thought about hastily getting dressed to try and find Lamia before she had to be at work, but she knew in her heart that would be futile because clearly Lamia wanted her space. Indeed, Michelle realized that Lamia was also probably hungry for sustenance that she simply couldn't give her. Wouldn't give her. Lamia had been in Michelle's carnivorous family before Michelle was even born. In fact, Lamia had lived much longer than any cat should live, and she'd never been sick. Michelle knew that Lamia would be safe now, even in New York City, as she'd proved the first time she escaped. So, slightly saddened but resolute, Michelle headed out to her second job as an exotic dancer a little while later.

About two hours into her second job, Michelle was fortunate enough to score champagne room private dances with an out-of-town businessman, or so he said; one could seldom believe most of what was said in a strip club. He'd tipped her well on stage, so she was expecting to make big bank in the champagne room. She thought he was creepy already though because when she'd been on all fours to collect bills from patrons at the end of the stage, he called her over to him with, "Here, Kitty Kitty."

After about an hour of dancing and drinking in the champagne room, the patron got up and left the club. Michelle was happy to see him go, and she thought no more about him as she continued to make money with the stage dances and more champagne room dances. Rather, her thoughts were on her cat Lamia. She knew she'd be okay now, but she already missed her.

Leaving the club much later, Michelle hailed a cab and was soon in front of her apartment building. She quickly paid the cabbie, including a big tip. And as the cab pulled away, much to her dismay, she heard a familiar voice say, "Here, Kitty Kitty." There he was: the creepy man from the bar with a menacing look on his face. Before she had time to even wonder how he knew where she lived, he placed a gun to her side and said, "Move quickly towards the grey car parked across the street if you want to live."

"How'd you know where I-I live?" Michelle stuttered somewhat, but trying not to let her fear get the best of her.

"I followed you home one night from the club whore...I'm not really an out-of-towner after all. In fact, I'd been hanging out at the club for months before you even noticed me. You probably never would have to this day if I hadn't started spending money on you."

True, Michelle thought, but she didn't dare stoke his fragile and clearly dangerous ego-fire. When they reached his grey car, on the sidewalk side, Michelle decided she'd have to act quickly to avoid getting in the car with him. She knew she'd probably be a goner if she did, so she figured she'd raise a ruckus, and he could shoot her if he liked, but she wasn't going to face a probably torturously slow death if she rode to an unknown somewhere in a probably deserted section of town with him. Right about as Michelle was going to break away and risk being shot, a grey blur shot across her right field of vision as she saw Lamia fix herself on the face of Michelle's assailant. He cried out in pain as Lamia's talons ripped across his face from the left side of his forehead diagonally down, taking

out his left eye in the process. Then Lamia proceeded to drain the blood and gore from his face with her fangs.

Lamia had ironically answered his call of "Here, Kitty Kitty."

And, knowing Lamia for what she really was, the finest vampire cat in all of *The Big Apple,* all Michelle could really think at that moment was that she was super glad her Lamia was no vegetarian.

S.O.B. Charlestonians

I looked back into the dark entranceway of the downtown church; I didn't see my mother, sister, sister-in-law, etc. Surely they wouldn't have left in the limo to return back to my mother's house on Legare Street without me. Breathing a sigh of relief, I saw my brother exit the church. "Where's mom?" I asked, when he was close enough to hear me without my shouting.

"I think they left."

"What?" I asked, confused. "We came with them."

"Yeah, well that's our ditzy mom." My brother said matter-of-factly.

***Ditzy, self-centered mom,* I thought. I shouldn't have been confused. Actually, leaving us behind was something pretty typical of her actions-wise. Or at least leaving me behind. In the past, she'd usually remembered my brother. At one time, I'd hated my brother, the only male born to my parents and definitely the favored golden child, but now I only felt sorry for him. Sorry that he had chosen/felt obligated to be forever trapped in downtown kiss-ass Charleston society. My being the Black Sheep (though I referred to**

myself as the Black Wolf so as to not sound so sheeple-like) was a blessing in disguise after all.

I only had to deal with rude, sense-of-entitlement Charlestonians with the *right* last name on rare occasions. Like at my dad's funeral when fugly, alcoholic Lolly Ravenel pushed her way past several people to get to me with, "Why, Leah Simmons, who are you with now? Husband number three?"

Not missing a beat, I said, looking her dead in the eye, "Yes. And, you… you still hitting the bottle hard?" But, before she could answer due to being so stunned, my brother grabbed my arm with a subdued smile and said, "Come with me. I'll see about getting us a ride," as he ignored Lolly Ravenel completely. I gladly followed him at that point. He confirmed my fears that we'd been left, but he said he'd already called a cab for us.

I thanked my brother, but I saw my ex-husband, #2, who remained single after our divorce and on good terms with me, so I decided to see if he'd give me a ride instead. Though I appreciated my younger brother's offer, I couldn't get over the fact that he was made executor of my father's will. Mom said it was because my brother was always there for her, but I knew that wasn't the case because so was my

sister, but she wasn't made executor, and she was also older than my brother. The case was simply this: my sister and I didn't have any gentleman's luggage dangling between our legs. My stupid whipped mother, a true victim of the wrong king of Southern upbringing, subconsciously thought males superior to females. Even in 2008! She was sexist, and it was against her own kind, and she was too weak to even realize it! No, she only prided herself on raising the finest South of Broad (S.O.B.) Charlestonian boy ever in my brother, while her heavy, guilt-ridden gold cross constantly wrapped itself like a noose around her neck.

Preeminent Parts

"You know you're very replaceable, right?!" The supermodel stated more than asked her ultra-dependable and homely personal assistant. The berated one who didn't model nude or sleep with old men for a living was struggling to carry all the boxes filled with gifts from her female boss' new sugar daddy. The supermodel was elated to be moving into his mansion, even though she wasn't alone. She, of course, had her poor personal assistant with her, and there were also twenty-three other well-kept supermodels living there...all with their own personal assistants, too. Only females lived in his mansion, except for the old Sugar Daddy himself, who prided himself on being all kinds of alpha male. Even though he could only get it up through the aid of pharmaceuticals at that point in his life.

....

The personal assistants all became close friends, helping each other out with their model bosses' high maintenance demands and some of the old sugar daddy's too. They were becoming more and more valuable by the day, due to their

ever-increasing skill-sets, including a general knowledge of how to get things done. Their models would have truly been lost without them. After all, there were ass bleaching appointments to be made, bikini waxing appointments, hair and nail appointments, and, most importantly, plastic surgery appointments to be made. All appointments were paid for by the way-past-his-prime sugar daddy. He spent millions on his high-paid model-whores yearly, while the certainly more practically valuable personal assistants received only a small salary. All the money spent was to make the supermodels more appealing for their magazine spreads and of course for their vaginal spreads in sugar daddy's bed.

• •

One day, the old man smiled in his mansion with glee, for he was expecting two dozen large packages there that day. When the doorbell rang, he quickly called the homely helpers (what he called the personal assistants as a pet name) to the front door. He needed their strength in lifting the packages to each of the supermodels' bedrooms. He was so excited he could barely stand it; he was practically jumping out of his slippers and smoking jacket! The stupid

supermodels figured their benevolent sugar daddy had given them each a large gift. Each heavy crate-like package measured six feet tall and was a little larger than the width of a regular sized human. What could possibly be inside? All the supermodels wondered, while flirting with their sugar daddy, saying he was a big tease for not telling them. The supermodels were sure that they were all about to receive the biggest gift they'd ever received from him. But the sugar daddy wouldn't divulge what was inside. He said he needed to get some things together first. It was then he went to his private chamber to make some well-planned calls.

• •

When the sugar daddy returned, he said that then was the perfect time for the crates to be opened. In fact, he'd given each of the personal assistants crowbars to pry them open. As it turns out, he, much like the supermodels, couldn't do very much by himself either. However, the very able personal assistants quickly pried the large boxes open to reveal 24 of the loveliest human female replicas they'd ever seen. They were lifelike to the touch, except for their skin felt even better than most humans, and their hair was more flawless, and their eyes, teeth, etc. all

more beautiful. And, if you didn't know any better, you'd swear they were actually real live supermodels when you turned on their voice boxes. They were the perfect androids, and even more perfect than humans. The sugar daddy danced around joyfully in his red robe (well, it was technically a smoking jacket, but it looked more like a hospital robe on someone his age). You see, he'd grown tired of his pretentious and expensive human supermodels. He simply didn't need them anymore now that the replacements had arrived. So, he said to the twenty-four supermodels gathered around him in shock, "Pack your bags, my dears, you've been replaced; I decided to upgrade." And, at that moment his doorbell rang again. It was the movers he'd called to come for the supermodels' things. Within the next two hours, the supermodels had been completely moved out, against their will and amidst many tears and angry reproaches. Yet, the sugar daddy asked the personal assistants to remain with him with, "You all are invaluable in the service arena. Even these female androids can't yet do what you do. Would you like to stay on and assist me?" The personal assistants were unanimous in their decision. They'd been thinking it over for a while…

Almost with one voice they said, "Thanks, but no thanks, we've decided to serve only ourselves from now on." And with that, they left the mansion, too, and shortly set up their own company. One that would eventually manufacture male androids for the likes of the wealthy and powerful women they decided to become.

The Final Frontier (An Explicit Sketch)

The hardest thing was getting the right light source. Getting the fiber optics molded into the latex was tricky at first. For one thing, the latex had to be reinforced; it was double the thickness of normal condoms. The idea of using a click on light was literally and figuratively brilliant; basically they were like the kind you see in bar necklaces given out on St. Patrick's Day, etc. The rest was relatively easy. The fiber optics ran down the length of the latex with a small computer chip also molded at the base that acted as a receiver. It transferred the images from the inner world for all to see...for the right price.

In a world of double penetration and more, the simple gaping asses scenes had been becoming a bit passé, so something more was being asked for. Porn hadn't been played out, but it was time for more ground-breaking, so to speak, inner space scenes to be filmed. Sure, there were people into the outer enhancement 3-D Virtual World enactment camp, but one ambitious porn director decided to make her mark in a different direction. Instead of focusing more on outside experience, she decided to film the inner experience instead. And she wasn't talking about any kind of inner spiritual experience!

Her condom cams have become quite the rage in both heterosexual and gay porn. Why just have gape when you can go into the canyon and see more? And there were three canyons, so to speak, that she was capitalizing on: ass, pussy and mouth. Two inner scenes available with a male performer and three with a female performer. Asses, pussies and mouths in pink, coral, brown, tan, red, purple, etc. And exciting spit falling scenes, like waterfalls scenes in the outer world, but there in oral sex inner cams scenes, while white and clear cum is streaking like rain over the condoms in the pussy inner shots and, finally, flat black worm-like streaks of feces sliding off from the ass-wall caverns, clearing out humans more than colonics can thanks to lots of lube. It's the new next level of inner-space-gonzo-porn watching. Mind-numbing new uncharted territory: it's what some futures are made of.

From Vegetarian to Vampire

I hated waiting tables: the rude customers, doling out the meat dishes, etc. But, I had nobody to speak of that I was really close to, except my pet pig, so I had to make sure I kept a roof over my head. I'd done okay for myself. I'd just turned 20 and had just bought my very own condo. And, I'd already had my little hybrid car for over two years. Besides spending time with my pig, I was pretty much a workaholic; in fact, I could even be accused of having *hyperopia*. You see, I wanted to make sure I'd never be at the mercy of an abuser again. In my case, the abuser was my father. My first memories were of when I was about three years old: I was being dangled over our second floor banister, held only by my father's hand on my ankle, because he thought it amusing. And, when he wanted to really turn up the fun meter, he'd let go of one ankle and catch the other. Never mind that I, his child, could have fallen to her death or be maimed, brain dead, etc. As it was, I'm sure it affected me emotionally. I certainly had a hard time getting close to men, for one, and for being scared, even when I perhaps should be, for two. I could have become a sadistic coward like my father easily, but I chose another route: helping those who couldn't help themselves, those who were like how I used to be. Those like animals. I became an animal rights activist, signing every petition I could, etc.

It was amazing I could feel anything really, as I was taught to never cry, even when I accidentally fell running up the stairs or something. I remember one time I was running up the stairs, fell down, skinned my right knee and started crying, like any child of around five years old would do. My crying disturbed my father, so he came marching over to me and said, "I want you to quit crying, apologize to the stairs and kiss them to make them better where you hurt them." Bastard! But as a child of only a half decade or so, I had no choice but to do what he said. I grew up secretly hating my parents, and who could blame me? I hated my father, and I hated my weak mother who let him get away with it. She was quick to point out every sinner's fault in her bible-thumping way, but she never realized her own. Bitch!

As soon as I secretly saved up enough money, I moved out of their place into a little efficiency apartment one town over. They had no idea where I was going; I made sure of that. There, in my little place, I lived the life of my dreams. Finally able to become the Vegetarian I'd always dreamed of being, and buying a baby piglet for a pet. The landlord didn't mind because I paid an extra $100.00 a month to be able to keep her there. As time went by, and I started working two waitressing jobs, I was able to save more and more money. Soon, I was able to afford my first condo. I was elated! My own place...well, after 15 years of monthly mortgage payments anyway. Unless I somehow managed to double up on payments or refinance or I had an unexpected windfall of some kind. Still, I couldn't believe how far I'd come~~~and I was very thankful to the forces that be. I was thinking something along those lines when a lovely middle-aged lady walked over to one of my tables and sat down. She sat down about dusk; she was to be my last table before going to my other job. So, I quickly went to take her order, to avoid getting out of there late. I wanted to be on time for my second job, too.

"Just water, thanks, and a salad."

Usually I don't like to get too personal with any of my customers, but something made me blurt out, "Are you a Vegetarian?"

She looked at me kind of strangely before answering, "No, no honey, I'm not. Kind of wish I was sometimes though."

"It's not that hard to become one," I volunteered, for some reason. "There are all kinds of vegetarian brands in the grocery stores now."

"Yes, I suppose so," she said smiling sweetly. I thought she must have been a knockout when she was younger, looking as good as she did at that point. I guess she must have been around 48 to 50 years old. I hadn't really ever dated anyone before, so I didn't actually know if I liked men or women or both. I was too busy surviving in an abusive household as a child and too busy working to keep my freedom as an adult. But, I thought I was kind of attracted to her; it was pretty much a new sensation to me. I was more surprised than anything.

As if reading my mind, she reached her hand out and touched my arm with, "Take as long as you like with my order sugar, I'm in no hurry." I felt my arm tingle where she'd touched me; I was definitely attracted to her. I had been so preoccupied with her presence that I'd barely noticed the large group of hayseeds, what we called rednecks, who come in shortly before she arrived. I didn't pay them much notice since they weren't seated in my section. But when they started making a major ruckus by refusing to pay their bill, then I certainly did. My customer looked at me warmly whispering, "those guys are assholes."

"I know," I said, running off to place her order. In about ten minutes, I returned with her order. Salads didn't take that long to fix. About that time, the hayseeds were exiting, having only paid for half their total order and leaving no tip.

When my lovely customer saw the guys leaving, I could swear she almost growled and then said, "Thank you, but I'm not hungry after all. Here honey, keep the change," she said throwing down a hundred dollar bill. I didn't care if she growled at the asshole guys or not. They were cheap dicks! Besides, with tipping me about $90.00, I'd have money to buy Bella, my pig, food for a month!

The next morning, as I headed out to my first job, I happened to hear the headline news on a radio station. I generally avoided the news, as it was filled with too much sadness for me to process with a full day and night of work ahead. However, that morning I heard that five guys were found mutilated six blocks from where I worked my second job. Their hearts were all ripped out and then drained of any blood within them. The victims were described as big, burly fellows. Not your average serial killer's targets. *That's funny,* I thought, *from their descriptions, they sound like the hayseeds that were at the restaurant last night.* Then, I worked all day, not having time to think any more about it.

Heading to my second job a little earlier than usual, I still thought nothing more about it as the sunsetting sky was just too beautiful to think of anything but it: it was almost as if the sky were bragging, boastfully sporting its splendid colors all at once. As if it were a pretty girl showing off her new eye-shadow pallet by covering her lids with every color all at once. I was watching the sky so intently that I almost missed the parking lot I generally parked in. Later, getting out of my car, I was startled to hear a voice right behind me say, "Careful, my dear, you shouldn't park too far away from your places of employment." I was more than a little surprised to see the good tipper I'd served yesterday. The one who'd left me the best tip ever and hadn't even touched her Vegetarian meal. Maybe she was just trying to give me a good tip of another kind, but I didn't especially like that one.

"Thanks," I muttered, "but I'm quite able to take care of myself." I didn't care if she had tipped me well or not. I didn't take bullshit off of anybody anymore.

"Good for you, my dear. I like a girl with some spunk." And, with that, she hurried across the parking lot and into the very restaurant I was going to work at. In fact, she was already seated in my section when I arrived.

Somewhat nonplussed, but trying to cover it up, I asked somewhat sarcastically, "Same thing as yesterday?" While I thought to myself, *Hope you're not some kind of creepy stalker, showing up to both my places of employment, even though they're across town from one another! Still, she's easy on the eyes. Well, my eyes at least. I'm not sure about the rest of the world.*

"Sure, Hon. A salad and water."

Right, I thought. I knew she said she wasn't a Vegetarian, but she must be a closet case one of some sort. And, in a way, I was right.

She left before touching any of her salad, or water either for that matter, and she generously gave me another $100.00 bill as well. At this rate, I'd have my mortgage payment paid before it was due. Still, something about her unsettled me, while at the same time, that *something* excited me.

Then, I did something totally unexpected after working my second job. Unexpected to me at least. I stopped in a seedier part of town and stopped at a sex store. I had no idea why at first, and then I got to the dildo section. Then, I found out why I'd been drawn there. A beautiful 6 inch (I was still a virgin, okay? So, anything bigger wouldn't have been appealing:) cyber skin cock. Kind of embarrassed, but not really, I purchased it. And, when I got back to my condo that night, I tried it out...all the while thinking about the pretty middle-aged lady. No accounting for tastes or actions after all I suppose.

I didn't have a landline phone. I thought they were mostly useless in the modern world when I already had a cell phone payment. Why did I want to pay an extra $50.00 a month just to say I had that, too? All I needed was my cell phone. As it was, I barely even used that. The only calls I generally got were from either of my two jobs, asking me to come in for employee meetings or cover someone else's shift. I hardly ever called in sick myself. But I was about to that night. Well, not technically sick, but something sickening. As it turns out, I was about to be eligible for a leave of absence, covered through bereavement. I'd received a call almost upon waking as my cell phone was also my alarm clock, and I kept it on the small bedside table next to my bed. I was very frugal. Anyway, I got a call from the police. Who knows how they'd tracked me down? I guess it wasn't really that difficult; I only lived one town over from my heinous parents. Make that heinous dead parents. I was told they'd been murdered, both their hearts ripped out and drained of any blood. Maybe I should say that I was sorry to hear the news. But, I wasn't. I just hoped the police weren't trying to track me down as a suspect. They weren't, however.

They said it looked like a serial killer. Probably male, from the brute strength of the crimes.

I decided to go to their evening funeral; evidently that was the only time they could be fit in for their funeral. It had been a busy time for the priest. Lots of people had been dying in his parish recently. So, I went to the funeral. More for appearances than anything, in case the police changed their mind about whom the suspect was. I was the only family they had there, but some of my mother's bible-thumping friends were there making a pitiful attention-grabbing scene of wringing their hands and looking up to their "savior" above mouthing *why?* It was disgusting! Then, I saw her. Sitting brazenly atop a headstone about 50 yards from where my parents were lowered for their final dirt nap. Her: the middle-aged beauty I was thinking about while pleasuring myself with the cyber skin penis. I know it was sick in a way, but I really just wanted to run over to her and talk. So, I did, right after I shook hands with the Episcopalian priest when the service for my parents ended.

I couldn't have been more surprised when I got about five yards from her, and she sprang off the tombstone with, "You're welcome." And then walked away. I was both stunned and

admiring of her figure as she merged into the shadows along the road up ahead.

What in the world did she mean? I didn't have long to think about it. I decided not to take my bereavement leave. After all, I wasn't bereaved; I was relieved. Right then and there at their funeral I could feel nothing but disgust for my biologicals. I flashed back to when my mother made me choose a live fish swimming in a restaurant tank for my dinner, knowing I preferred not eating meat of any kind.

It was served up on my plate with its dead eyes staring at me as if to say, *Murderer, why'd you choose me?* My mother just laughed as I ran to the restaurant bathroom to throw up. She was always telling me to toughen up, yet she was never tough enough to stand up to my dad. Come to think of it, they were both really abusive and cold. But, now, my parents could no longer hurt me. And, I knew I'd make more money working than leave pay because of my tips. So, I headed to my second job, after changing in my little car.

My first customers at my second job were gross; they ordered their steaks rare with bacon added as a side-order. I almost wished they'd have a heart attack right then and there to spare the life of more cows and pigs. Shortly afterwards, they left, leaving me only a $1.00 tip on their $40.00 bill; they ended up getting dessert too. Thank goodness no more animals were killed for that part of their meal at least.

Later, I had to walk about three blocks away to my little hybrid; there wasn't a spot for me in the parking lot since I'd arrived late for my shift, due to attending my parents' funeral. When I was about 50 yards away, I heard a scream on my left, then a loud thud. Scared, but not wanting to not help someone truly in need, I approached the dark alleyway on my left. I clutched my keys in my right hand with the largest car key protruding from between my pointer and middle fingers. Not that it was really a weapon, but it was something I figured. If I'd only known what I was to be up against, then even a gun wouldn't have been great protection. But, I really had no idea.

Entering the alleyway, I saw two figures curled up on the asphalt. As I cautiously walked closer, I saw with horror that they were the husband and wife customers I'd just served at the restaurant. The steak and bacon ones. Only, it now looked like they'd been someone's meal as their hearts had clearly been ripped out of their bodies. Fighting the urge to throw-up, I noticed something move quickly out of the corner of my right eye. And, suddenly, there she was…again.

"Hey Sugar," she said, her eyes glowing a strange reddish-black in the moonlight above. Then I saw them: her fangs, still bloody from her last meal.

"You did this?" I asked incredulously.

"Yes."

"But why?"

"Because you didn't like them, and I was thirsty."

"Are you still thirsty?"

"Maybe a little."

"Are you thirsty for *me*?"

"Yes, but in a different way."

"I-I don't understand," I began.

"Look, it's not safe here," she said, looking down at the bodies she'd just mutilated. "Let's go for a ride, and I'll explain everything."

"I've got to get home to feed my pig, Bella," I replied, caring more for my pig's life than my own at that point.

"Fine. Bella and you will be fine."

"I'll talk as you drive." So, that's what we did. But that was just the start of our existence together. She turned me that very night. And, though I could have looked at it as a sad plight for I was to spend the rest of my existence surviving

off of only blood as a former Vegetarian, I chose not to because I realized I could actually even the playing field for animals and humans as I drained only the meat-eating humans ever after. Plus, I had so much money from robbing them after killing them that I paid off my small condo within the year and was able to buy a large house in the country with *her* where we started a farm for rescued animals, including cows, pigs, chickens, etc.

Lucas McPherson has been an avid reader and writer from her childhood on; currently, she has a book review column titled "Lucas McPherson's Literary Lair" at *Psychic Times International.* Her short story included within this book and titled "What Really Happened in the Labyrinth" was recently featured in Psychic Times International (Fall 2009 Issue) at http://www.voicesfrombeyond7.com/PsychicTimesWelcome.html. "What Really Happened in the Labyrinth" also appeared in The Witches Digest (Samhain 2009 Issue) at http://www.witchesdigest.co.uk/new/. When not reading, writing, interviewing and reviewing movies as well, Lucas enjoys long walks in the woods, playing with her fur kids, working out with her husband to various exercise videos, lifting weights and competing in 5K road races. Feel free to send a friend request to Lucas on her MySpace page at http://www.myspace.com/authorlucasmcpherson.

Cyan Jenkins began drawing comics before she learned to spell. Throughout her education she has illustrated for various types of books and took commissions for portrait work. Her first published book was Bunkie the Turtle a childrens book. Soon after, she illustrated Beyond the Eyes. Which is a book of poems. She received her Bachelors degree in Fine Art from Ringling College of Art and Design, majoring in Illustration with a minor in Visual Development. She continues to freelance and work as the Art Director of Target Audience Magazine. Her freelance work includes comics, childrens books, animated storyboards (animatics), layout design, and just about anything you want to "throw her way." You can find her work at CyanJenkins.blogspot.com